The Pocket Mommy

By **RACHEL EUGSTER** *Illustrated by* **TOM GOLDSMITH**

TUNDRA BOOKS

Samuel clutched his mother's hand as he walked to kindergarten. His feet felt heavier with every step.

"Mommy," he said, "I hate it when you leave me at school. I wish you were the tiniest mommy in the world, so I could keep you in my pocket all day."

"Oh, Samuel," said Mommy. "I hate leaving you, too. But guess what? I've got a tiny mommy right here. Let me tuck her in."

As Samuel held open his pocket, his mom pretended to slip something inside. Then she gave him a big hug good-bye, and was gone.

"Circle Time!" Mrs. Dupree called. Samuel joined his classmates in the circle. His pocket felt heavy. And warm. And wiggly. He peered inside – and gasped.

At the bottom of Samuel's pocket was a teeny, tiny mommy. She gave him a cheery wave.

"But– but– " Samuel stuttered. "You're real?"

"Sure!" the Pocket Mommy called, in a pocket-sized voice. "I'm here to help!"

Samuel was speechless.

The Pocket Mommy started helping right away.

In Circle Time, Samuel couldn't remember the words to the song.

"I can help!" said the Pocket Mommy. She stood on his shoulder and sang along.

During Alphabet Time, Samuel wasn't sure how to write his name.

"I can help!" said the Pocket Mommy, and she acted out the shape of each letter.

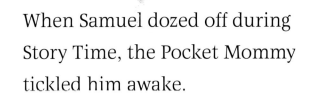

When Samuel dozed off during Story Time, the Pocket Mommy tickled him awake.

And when Samuel couldn't remember what cows say, the Pocket Mommy helped again.

"MOOOOO!" she bellowed, right into his ear.

After Snack Time, the children worked on their farm mural. Samuel drew a sheep. When his elbow bumped the purple crayon, it plopped to the floor and rolled under the bookcase.

"I'll get it!" said the Pocket Mommy. She slid down the table leg and slithered under the bookcase.

"*Oof, omph, mmrmph*," she grunted, as she disappeared.

"Got it!" she called.

The crayon rolled back out, followed by a very grubby Pocket Mommy.

Samuel picked a spider web out of her hair.

"Maybe next time I'll get it myself," he said.

"Time to cut out our animals," called Mrs. Dupree.

"Be careful to cut along the lines," the Pocket Mommy said.

Samuel gave her a look.

"Hmm," she said. "I'm not sure about the shape of that sheep."

"Mommy," Samuel said, "I can do it myself!"

"Fine," said the Pocket Mommy. "I'll find something else to do." She climbed over the edge of the table and slipped down the leg.

Samuel cut around the last little bit of sheep.

Across the room, the Pocket Mommy clambered onto the blackboard ledge.

"What a mess!" she said. She grabbed a paintbrush and began to sweep. Chalk dust rose in energetic swirls and rained onto the floor.

Samuel raised his eyebrows. "Hey!" he said. "Slow down there."

"Don't worry," said the Pocket Mommy. "I'm just cleaning up." She gave Samuel a jaunty salute with the paintbrush.

Samuel put tiny glue dots onto the back of the sheep.
The Pocket Mommy scaled the bookshelves.

"These books need a good sorting," she declared.
"Stays, stays, *goes*. Stays, stays, *goes*." With every "goes,"
she gave one book a hearty push. A book avalanche
began to cascade across the floor.

"Be careful, Mommy," said Samuel. "That's not a good idea."

"Nonsense! I'm making it better," said the Pocket
Mommy cheerfully. She heaved another book off the shelf.

Samuel pressed his sheep onto the mural. The Pocket Mommy shinnied up to the countertop and eyed the guinea pig.

"What a pig sty!" She opened the cage door and brandished her brush. "Out, out, *out*!"

Samuel ran across the room. "Mommy, no!"

The Pocket Mommy poked him with
the brush. Samuel grabbed it.
The Pocket Mommy whirled it away.
It whizzed around and whacked
Samuel right across the nose.

"Ow!" cried Samuel. "That's it!" He stuffed
the Pocket Mommy into his pocket.

The pocket wriggled like an angry bee. "*Xmpfl*," it buzzed. "*Fzzl, spxfbz!*"

"Quiet!" said Samuel. "You are having a Time Out."

"Harumph!" grumped the pocket.

A few minutes later, Samuel peeked inside. The Pocket Mommy was fast asleep.

She woke up when Mrs. Dupree called the kids to make papier-mâché animals.

"Ooh!" said the Pocket Mommy. "I can help. I know lots about papier-mâché!" She climbed out of Samuel's pocket, down his arm, and onto the can of flour.

"Wait!" Samuel called. "You are still in a Time Out."

"Pour in the water!" commanded the Pocket Mommy, standing tippy-toe on the rim.

"Mommy! Get down! That's very danger–"

"Aieee!" the Pocket Mommy cried, as she teetered and tottered and tipped into the can.

"Yikes!" gulped Samuel. He reached into the can, fished out the struggling Pocket Mommy, and stood her on the table.

The Pocket Mommy was covered in flour. Samuel tried to blow it gently away. It didn't help. There was flour in the Pocket Mommy's hair. There was flour all over her clothes. There was flour in her itty-bitty shoes. When she opened her mouth to speak, all that came out was a tiny white puff.

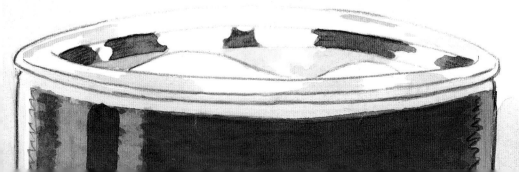

"Mommy," said Samuel, "this isn't working."

"But I'm only trying to help!" spluttered the Pocket Mommy.

"I know," said Samuel. "But look what happened! You made a book avalanche. You misbehaved with the guinea pig. And you almost got papier-mâché'd! I didn't know that a pretend mommy could get into so much trouble!"

The Pocket Mommy hung her head. "I'm sorry," she said. "I guess you don't need my help, after all."

"Clean-up time, children!" called Mrs. Dupree. "Your parents will be here soon to take you home."

"Tell you what," said the Pocket Mommy, "I'll get myself cleaned up. Then I'll take care of all this flour. You get ready to go home."

"Are you sure you can manage on your own?" asked Samuel.

"Absolutely," said the Pocket Mommy, seizing her paintbrush. "This is child's play."

"All right!" Samuel said, and he ran across the room.

As he reached his cubby, his mother arrived. Samuel gave her a huge hug.

"Mommy!" he said. "I am so glad to see you."

"I'm happy to see you, too," she said. "Did you have a good day?"

"You won't believe it!" said Samuel. "Come and see." He pulled his mom over to the table.

There he found a tidy pile of flour. The paintbrush lay across the empty flour can. But there was no sign of the Pocket Mommy.

"That's funny," Samuel said. "She was here a minute ago."

"Who was?" asked Mommy.

"The Pocket Mommy," said Samuel. "She was here all day."

Mommy smiled. "Did it help to have a pretend mommy with you?"

"At first," said Samuel. "But then I spent the whole day rescuing her."

Mommy laughed. "Would you like me to give you another pretend mommy tomorrow?"

Samuel thought about it. "You know what, Mommy? Maybe I just need you to do your mommying at home."

Mommy held out her hand. "Shall we go, then?"

Samuel grinned. "I'm ready," he said.

And off they went.

For Jay, for Aaron, and especially for Samuel, who made this wish. —R.E.

For Emily and Gord. —T.G.

Text copyright © 2013 by Rachel Eugster
Illustrations copyright © 2013 by Tom Goldsmith

Published in Canada by Tundra Books, a division of Random House of Canada Limited,
One Toronto Street, Suite 300, Toronto, Ontario M5C 2V6

Published in the United States by Tundra Books of Northern New York,
P.O. Box 1030, Plattsburgh, New York 12901

Library of Congress Control Number: 2012948450

Library and Archives Canada Cataloguing in Publication

Eugster, Rachel
The pocket mommy / by Rachel Eugster ; illustrated by
Tom Goldsmith.

ISBN 978-1-77049-300-1. – ISBN 978-1-77049-498-5 (EPUB)

I. Goldsmith, Tom II. Title.

PS8609.U58P63 2013   jC813'.6   C2012-906122-0

We acknowledge the financial support of the Government of Canada through the Canada Book Fund and that of the Government of Ontario through the Ontario Media Development Corporation's Ontario Book Initiative. We further acknowledge the support of the Canada Council for the Arts and the Ontario Arts Council for our publishing program.

ONTARIO ARTS COUNCIL
CONSEIL DES ARTS DE L'ONTARIO

The artwork in this book was rendered in graphite, watercolor and colored pencil.

www.tundrabooks.com

Printed and bound in China

1 2 3 4 5 6   18 17 16 15 14 13